MORRIS AND BORIS
AT THE
CIRCUS

An I Can Read Book®

MORRIS AND BORIS AT THE CIRCUS

BY B. WISEMAN

HarperCollins*Publishers*

Morris and Boris at the Circus
Copyright © 1988 by Bernard Wiseman

Library of Congress Cataloging-in-Publication Data
Wiseman, Bernard.
  Morris and Boris at the circus.

  (An I can read book)
  Summary: Morris and Boris go to the circus as
spectators and end up being part of the action.
  [1. Moose—Fiction. 2. Bears—Fiction.
3. Circus—Fiction] I. Title. II. Series.
PZ7.W7802Mk 1988   [E]   87-45682
ISBN 0-06-026477-2
ISBN 0-06-026478-0 (lib. bdg.)
ISBN 0-06-444143-1 (pbk.)

For my boys,
and children of ALL ages!

"I saw a circus,"

said Boris the Bear.

"Did it see you?"

asked Morris the Moose.

"No," said Boris.

"Why?" asked Morris.

"Were you hiding?"

8

"No," said Boris.

"I was not hiding."

"Was the circus sleeping?"

asked Morris.

9

"No!" cried Boris.

"The circus does not SLEEP!"

"It must get very tired,"

Morris said.

"NO!" shouted Boris.

"The circus does not get tired!

The circus is...

Oh, never mind.

I will show you

what the circus is."

Boris said,

"That is the circus tent.

It is called the Big Top.

And that is—"

"I know," said Morris.

"That is the Big Bottom!"

"No!" said Boris.

"That is an elephant."

13

"That is a clown,"

said Boris.

Morris cried,

"The poor clown!

He must have a cold.

His nose is red."

"No," said Boris.

"That is not his real nose.

He stuck it on."

"But it makes him look funny,"

said Morris.

"Everyone will laugh at him!"

15

"Clowns WANT to look funny,"

said Boris.

"Look!

Those are lions and tigers

and horses and trained dogs."

"Where are the MOOSE?"

Morris asked.

17

"There are no moose

in the circus," said Boris.

Morris cried,

"Moose SHOULD be in the circus!"

"Tell the Ringmaster," said Boris.

"He is a man in a big hat.

Let's go find him."

18

"Ringmaster," said Morris,

"moose should be in the circus!"

"Why not?" said the Ringmaster.

"Go into the Big Top, moose.

Go be in the circus!"

The Ringmaster yelled,

"Here are the Great Gambinis!

They ride horses bareback!"

"I do not have a horse,"

said Morris.

"But I can ride BEAR-back!"

21

"Not on my back!" cried Boris.

"Go be an animal tamer.

Get in the cage

with the lions and tigers."

22

"Look," said Morris.

"PART of me is in the cage."

23

"ALL of you must go in!"

Boris shouted.

"Will all of me come out?"

asked Morris.

"Yes," said Boris.

"If you make the big cats
listen to you."

25

Morris said,

"Listen to me,

lions and tigers!

Please BE GOOD.

Please DO NOT BITE!"

"No! No!" cried Boris.

"Look at the animal tamer.

Use your tail like a whip.

Tell them to do something!"

"Lions and tigers!"

yelled Morris.

"Look at my tail.

DO something!"

"Ohhh!

Come out of the cage!"

cried Boris.

"Go try to walk

like the trained dogs."

"Oh, get up!" said Boris.

"Try to bow like the dogs."

33

"You mean BOW-WOW,"

said Morris.

"No!" cried Boris.

"I do not mean bow-wow!

I mean bow with no wow.

Bend over like the dogs.

That is how to wow. No!

I mean, how to bow-wow.

No! Ohhh—don't wow!"

"Climb the ladder!" Boris shouted.

"Be a high-wire walker."

"Can I be a LOW-wire walker?"

asked Morris.

37

"Grrrrr!" growled Boris.

"I will be a HIGH-wire walker," said Morris.

Morris put one hoof

on the wire.

"Put your other hoof

on the wire!" yelled Boris.

"No! No!" Boris cried.

"Put both hoofs on it

at the same time!

40

"Come down!" Boris shouted.

"Go blow a horn with the seals.

Try to make music!"

"Did I make music?"

Morris asked a seal.

"It sounded more like MOOSE-SICK!"

said the seal.

"Come on," said Boris.

"Try to be an acrobat."

"Do you see the seesaw?"

asked Boris.

"You stand on the low end.

I will jump down

onto the high end.

Then you will fly up

into that chair."

"Oh, no," said Morris.

"That chair is HIGH.

Only babies sit in HIGH chairs!"

"GRRRRR!" growled Boris.

"Maybe you can be a clown.

Come on—

I will get you clown clothes.

I will paint your nose."

48

"Why do you have to

paint my nose?"

asked Morris.

"I told you why!"

cried Boris.

"Clowns do not show

their real noses.

Clowns put on red roses.

I mean, clowns do not show

their real roses.

Clowns put on real noses!

No! No! Ohhh—come on!"

"HERE!" growled Boris.

"Put on these clown clothes.

Put on those big shoes."

"Ohhh," said Morris.

"The clown clothes will not fit.

I am not fat.

But the shoes will fit.

Look at my foot!

See the big toes?"

"ARRRRR!" roared Boris.

"Foot on the clown clothes!

I mean, PUT on the clown toes!

No! No! Ohhh—GET DRESSED!"

"Now I will paint your nose,"
said Boris.

"I will help you," said Morris.

"It is a big job!"

"We are done," said Boris.

"Now go and be a clown."

"How?" asked Morris.

"Here," said Boris.

"Take this clown umbrella.

Squeeze the bottom."

"Like this?" asked Morris.

"ARRRRRRRRRRR!" roared Boris.

"I WILL GET YOU!"

"Moose," said the Ringmaster.

"You are not

a good bareback rider,

or animal tamer,

or trained dog,

or acrobat,

or high-wire walker,

and you cannot blow a horn

and make music.

But you are a FUNNY CLOWN!

You made everybody laugh!"

"No!" Boris cried.

"He didn't make ME laugh!"